Metaphorosis

January 2019

Beautifully made speculative fiction

Also from Metaphorosis Books

Reading 5X5: Readers' Edition
Reading 5X5: Writers' Edition

Best Vegan Science Fiction & Fantasy

Best Vegan SFF of 2017
Best Vegan SFF of 2016

Metaphorosis Magazine

Metaphorosis: Best of 2018
Metaphorosis: Best of 2017
Metaphorosis: Best of 2016
Metaphorosis 2018: The Complete stories
Metaphorosis 2017: The Complete stories
Metaphorosis 2016: Nearly Complete Stories
Monthly issues

by B. Morris Allen

Susurrus
Allenthology: Volume I
Tocsin: and other stories
Start with Stones: collected stories
Metaphorosis: a collection of stories

Metaphorosis

January 2019

edited by
B. Morris Allen

Metaphorosis Books

Neskowin

ISSN: 2573-136X (online)
ISBN: 978-1-64076-131-5 (e-book)
ISBN: 978-1-64076-132-2 (paperback)

January 2019

The Book of Regrets

M.J. Gardner

Christmas Eve, 2014, Cobourg, Ontario, Canada

When Craig came into the living room with two steaming mugs of hot mulled cider, Adam had already moved the small pile of Christmas gifts from under the tree to the ottoman that doubled as a coffee table. The room smelled of wood smoke and pine and now cinnamon and apples. A two-storey window showed the deep blue Lake silvered by the moon under a black sky. The moon, candles twinkling on the window sill, the tree lights, and the fire were the only light in the room.

"This is perfect," sighed Craig as he settled on the couch next to Adam.

"Now that we have achieved perfection, can we open our presents?"

Tomorrow was Christmas, but they would be on a plane to Cuba. Craig didn't want to haul the gifts to Cuba and back, and worse, opening Christmas gifts in a tropical climate, instead of in cold, snowy Cobourg, just seemed wrong to him.

"Yes! Are you finished packing?"

"What's to pack?" Adam picked up a present from the pile, one he had placed on top so he could open it first. "All I need is a Speedo and a toothbrush."

"No, no, that one is for last." Craig took the present out of Adam's hand and put it on the farther side of the ottoman.

It was clearly a book, wrapped at the shop in acid-free, brown paper which Craig had tried to Christmas-up with a red ribbon. Adam had already shaken it, felt it, and sniffed it. It had the delightfully musty smell of a used bookstore.

"What if I want to open it first?"

"Well, you can't."

"But what if I do?"

Craig put his hand against Adam's jaw and gently turned his head to give him a kiss. "You can't, love. I forbid it."

"You forbid it!" laughed Adam. "Oh, well!"

"Yes, I forbid it! Now, here, open this one."

Adam looked at the tag. "It's socks."

"Yes, of course it's socks. Why does your aunt always send you socks?"

"To keep my feet warm."

Craig rolled his eyes. "Of course."

They made their way through the packages. A generic drug store manly shower kit from Craig's brother, a bottle from Tom, the in-the-closet priest, chocolates from Adam's niece, matching ugly Christmas sweaters from his sister, and from Craig's mother a lovely Chinese puzzle box containing a bag of homegrown marijuana and a check.

"Now you can open the book—I mean—that gift, love," announced Craig.

"No, no, you said last. Here."

"What's this?"

"My gift to you."

Craig turned the envelope over in his hand. "You got me a card?"

"Yes, just a card. Five years is paper, right?"

Craig opened the card and took out the folded piece of paper.

"What is this?"

"I got the Jag restored."

"What? But, it was a write-off!"

Adam nodded. He felt smug and he was sure he deserved to feel smug. "You never thought about what happened after the insurance company paid you off? They kept the car."

"Well, yes, I suppose that makes sense."

"They auctioned it off for peanuts, and I went and bought it at the auction, and took it there," he pointed at the International Motors letterhead on the receipt. Adam had blacked out all the prices. "I said, how much to put this back together?"

"You're kidding me!"

"It won't be done for another week or two. You need the receipt to pick it up."

"Oh my God, Adam!" Craig threw his arms around Adam and kissed him till he struggled to get loose.

"I want to open my book!"

"Oh, I feel bad. This is so wonderful! How much did this cost? And all I got you was another book."

Adam scoffed. "A car is just a way to get around. Books are life."

As eager as he had been to get to it, Adam opened the parcel carefully. The acid-proof paper made him cautious. Books were life, but some were also investments.

The book was old. Adam could feel the strings of the binding through the spine, like the bones beneath the skin of an old cat. The burgundy leather binding had faded to pink at the corners and on the ribs of the spine. The gold leaf title had worn off, but the impression in the leather was still legible: *The Book of Regrets*.

The pages were yellow; the corners brittle. Inside, the first page was blank, and after that was the hand-lettered title, *The Book of Regrets*, done with a quill pen and black ink that had turned rusty and stained a mirror image on the verso of the flyleaf. On the next page was the same handwriting and the same ink.

I regret cheating my cousin out of his inheritance.

Jebediah Stone, Upper Canada, 1798

"Where did you get this?"

"At a book shop in Hull called *Petit Adam.*"

"*Petit Adam?*"

"With a name like that I could hardly not go and check it out, could I?"

"Thank you." Adam caressed the leather and resisted the urge to put the book to his nose. Craig teased him for smelling books. "This is going to go in the barrister bookcase."

"I'm going to go and tidy up the kitchen," said Craig.

The kitchen was already tidy: Adam had cleaned up after dinner. He didn't argue, though. Craig, his stainless steel kitchen, and cleanliness were a holy trinity.

Adam opened the book randomly, and read the regrets of Margaret Anne Killian, aged sixty-seven. She had a lot of them. She had apparently been storing them up. She regretted not hugging and kissing her father good-bye before he went off to the war when she was four. She regretted pushing someone named Annabelle Lee off a merry go round. She regretted letting Bruce Harvey kiss her in the cloak room because she gave him an inch and he took a mile that he didn't deserve and which she would rather have saved for her wedding night. She regretted poisoning her sister's cat, because, although her sister deserved it, the cat did not. She regretted letting the hospital whisk her second baby away from her, sight unseen. If it was going to die anyway, she would rather have held it at least once. She regretted not going to see the Beatles when they were in Toronto. She regretted marrying a second time and was happy to be a widow again. She regretted growing old, but, she supposed, there was nothing she could do about that.

There were blank pages between some of the regrets. Barry Keane regretted always playing it safe and never taking chances. Eachern Jacobs regretted not following his father into the family business. Sheldon McIlvey regretted shooting an Indian boy, even if they were thieves and beggars and illegally camping on his land.

Mary Alice Leahorn Wright regretted having a baby out of wedlock and giving it up for adoption, while Louise Lawson regretted going to college and pursuing a career instead of getting married and having a family, and Marie Anne Beauchamp regretted giving up her nursing career to get married and have children.

Ivan Horn regretted letting his sister have the family silver.

Adam looked out at the water. The moon was high now, out of sight above the roof. He didn't have any regrets. How could he possibly be unhappy? He was legally (finally!) married to his lover, living in a fabulous house on the edge of Lake Ontario. He worked a comfortable two days a week in Kingston and performed wedding ceremonies on weekends throughout the year. Life was good. Like Margaret Ann Killian, he regretted growing old, but, as the joke went, it was better than the alternative.

"There," announced Craig, "we're all ready for tomorrow. Assuming you're packed. Are you packed?"

"Yes. I told you: a Speedo and a toothbrush."

"You might also want your passport. I'm going to bed."

"I'll be there in a few minutes. I have to tuck my new treasure in for the night."

Adam took *The Book of Regrets* into his office and rummaged around in his desk for his acid-free pens. It felt naughty to write something new into an antique like this, but the book's empty pages demanded it. It was what made it unique and valuable—that every owner had contributed to it. He wasn't going to be left out.

Adam stared at the blank, yellowed page for some time, and then wrote, "I regret not becoming a writer."

He signed and dated the entry, blew on the ink, unnecessarily, to make sure it was dry before closing it, and then locked the book into the barrister bookcase.

Christmas Day, 1972, New Liskeard, Ontario, Canada

Adam woke to the sound of cows lowing in the barn. Cows with uncomfortably heavy udders that needed to be milked. The first pale yellow of dawn glittered in the frost on the inside of his bedroom window. It was cold. He reluctantly peeled back the covers and slipped out of bed. It was his job to get the fire going in the stove that had burnt down to embers overnight.

The floor was cold on his feet despite his wool socks. Why was everything so big? He felt like Alice in Wonderland after drinking the shrinking potion.

Maybe he was dreaming.

The cold air made him need to pee. He ran down the hall to the bathroom, which was also out-of-scale-large, and looked in the mirror.

A boy's unlined face stared back at him: blue eyes and straight white-blond hair. Shock doused him like cold water and he peed down the leg of his pajama pants. He was awake now. Wide awake. He was not dreaming this: it was too vivid.

He was home.

He was in the farmhouse in New Liskeard.

Adam blinked at himself and reached out to touch his reflection in the mirror. He was ten years old again.

"Get out of the way," ordered his sister Eleanor.

Adam stared at her. She was twelve years old, a skinny girl with braids and a flannel nightgown. Her feet drummed out a rhythm on the cold tile.

"I have to pee!" She pushed him out of the bathroom and closed the door. Through its wooden panels Adam heard her make a disgusted noise. She had just stepped in his puddle of pee.

Adam ran back to the bedroom and took a look at it. There was the high bed that he shared with his older brother, covered in a threadbare patchwork quilt; the old dresser that would be worth a couple hundred in a shop now; his brother's larger maple dresser; the bead board paneling on the walls painted cream; and his brother John staring back at him.

"What?" demanded John.

"I'm ten," Adam squeaked.

"No kidding, dunderhead."

Right, okay, so John was thirteen, really thirteen.

"If you want to live to be eleven, go get the stove going."

Adam took a step forward and his sock squelched. He pulled it off. He was so limber! And so small. The bed was like a mountain and Adam had to climb onto it.

Ten years old.

Ten! Years! Old!

"What are you doing, dunderhead?" crabbed John. "Go stoke the fire so we can get up and open our presents."

"Fuck off." Adam's voice came out piping and sweet as a songbird's.

"What!? I'm going to tell Mama you swore."

"Go milk the cows," Adam said, just to test out his voice again. Had he really sounded like that as a child? His voice held no authority at all; no wonder his siblings bossed him around.

"Go milk the cows," called their mother from down the hall. "The cows still need milking, even on Christmas."

His brother got out of bed with a growl. "Dunderhead," he shot at Adam, as if it were his fault the cows needed milking. Adam had forgotten that his brother used to call him that.

"And Adam, you watch your mouth."

"Yes, ma'am." Adam suppressed a giggle at the sound of his own voice. At the absurdity of it all.

He must be dreaming. But it was too vivid, too detailed. He could read the titles on the spines of the books on his bedside table. You weren't supposed to be able to read in dreams.

Ten years old.

He still had puberty ahead of him. He peeked inside his pajama bottoms to be sure, and yes, he was hairless down there. And wet. He peeled the PJs off and stood shivering.

Out the window, the fields were flat and white with snow, like the blank page of a book, like his life, unwritten, there for him to do over again. Assuming he didn't wake up and find that this was just a dream, there were things he could do differently. He wasn't going to let his brother bully him, for one thing, and he wasn't going to wait so long to come out.

What else? What did he really...

Regret.

The Book of Regrets.

"Adam?"

Had it sent him back here to relive his life, to change things? Over a simple comment that he hadn't become a writer? Not to put things right that had once gone wrong, or some such grandiose nonsense? He wasn't supposed to stop Hitler or keep JFK form being assassinated, was he?

No, those things were in the past. It was 1972 and he was ten years old.

"Adam," called his mother sharply, and fifty-two or not, Adam snapped to attention. "What are you doing?"

The fire. Stoke the fire. His job, every morning. Adam wrestled open a dresser drawer. "I'm coming!"

Christmas Eve, 2014, New York City, New York, USA

Adam looked out at New York. He couldn't look down on it from his $2 million flat, but he didn't have to look up either. At night, New York glittered, but now, in the grey, slushy afternoon it was bleak and dull.

He had bought the flat at the height of his success, after the book about Stonewall and just when his book about AIDS hit the market. He was credited with blowing open the whole AIDS thing, frightening people—necessarily—with what would happen if the gay community ignored it, if the media labeled it a gay disease, and if medical science didn't do the responsible thing. Only Adam knew how many people he had saved.

A reviewer once described him as prescient. His stock advisor thought the same thing.

But now that prescience had run out. He was back to where he started: December 24, 2014, when *The Book of Regrets* had sent him back in time to change his life. And he had changed it. Drastically.

That path had taken him places he had not been before. He had become an American citizen. He had won a Pulitzer and been listed for a Nobel. He could write any drivel and have publishers in a bidding war over it. It had resulted in many interesting relationships, with men and women, but none that lasted, none with depth. Christmas Eve and he was alone.

He had never crossed paths with Craig. When they should have met, when they had met originally, he was living with the Kurds in Afghanistan. Sweet little Craig with his shaved head and fuzzy little soul patch, his sparkling clean stainless steel kitchen, his absolute inability to decorate, and his devotion to his morning jog no matter what the weather was like.

The house in Cobourg was a lifetime away.

Adam's book collection was more compact and select than in his previous life; many of the volumes warranted being under lock and key. But there was one he did not have: *The Book of Regrets*. He had never come across it.

Where had Craig said he'd found it? Oh, right, *Petit Adam*, how could he forget a name like that? In Ottawa? Or was it Toronto? Gawd, that conversation was forty-two years ago! Adam pulled out his phone and Googled it. Hull. Six hours and fifty-one minutes away on the I-81.

With no Adam in his life to buy it for, Craig would not have bought the book, probably never have gone into the shop at all, and it would still be sitting there the day after Boxing Day. Adam packed a bag, gave the parking valet $20 for bringing his car out from the underground garage and headed for the highway. After all, there was nothing—and no one—to keep him in New York over the holiday season.

Through the long hours of Christmas Day and Boxing Day, Adam read and fidgeted and watched porn on his phone. When *Petit Adam* opened at ten on December 27, he was waiting outside, with the cold rising from the packed snow of the sidewalk right through the leather soles of his shoes.

"*Bon matin,*" greeted the owner.

"I am looking for a book."

"Well, you are in the right place," laughed the man. His accent was Trinidadian, overlaid with Quebecois.

"It's called *The Book of Regrets.*"

The owner stopped and frowned. "That is funny. That book sits on the shelf for months and no one looks at it. Christmas Eve, I sold it, and here you are asking about it now."

"Sold it to whom?"

"You know, you look familiar."

Adam wanted to turn the man upside down and shake him until the name and address of the person he had sold *The Book of Regrets* to fell out of his pockets like loose change. Instead, he stepped forward and extended his hand. "Adam Bovenkamp. I'm an author. You may have heard of me."

"Oh, goodness! It is an honour to have you in my shop."

"I need to get my hands on that book."

"The man who bought it, I do not know him. He paid cash." The owner shrugged. "I am sorry."

It was Craig. It had to be Craig. Adam's timeline had changed, but Craig's hadn't.

"Monsieur, would you sign....?"

Only one way to find out.

Adam walked out of the shop, checked out of the Chateau Laurier, left Ottawa, and drove to tiny Grafton. There he turned right down the little two-lane road that ran towards slightly larger Cobourg. Yes, there was the house, just like he remembered it. Smoke was wafting from the chimney.

It had been forty years since he had been here, but pulling into the driveway something slammed into him like an avalanche. It was the feeling of coming home. Adam put his foot on the brake and just breathed. This feeling, this was something he had not felt in a very long time. He did not feel it in his New York apartment, not like this. And when his mother had been alive (for the second time) and he had gone back to the farmhouse in New Liskeard to visit, his feelings were more complicated.

When he recovered from the initial impact, Adam continued up the drive and parked behind a Lexus. No Jag.

A stranger answered the door. Tall, salt-and-pepper hair, hand-knit merino wool sweater in tweedy grey. Adam immediately knew two things—that salt & pepper man was gay, and that he hated him.

"Hello, I'm, uh, looking for Craig."

"Craig!" called the man. "He's just upstairs. Come in, let me close the door. Sorry, I don't want to let the cat out."

Adam recognized the thump of Craig's feet on the stairs above his head and he held his breath. Craig came around the corner wearing a matching hand-knit sweater in tweedy brown. He had a mustache and goatee instead of the little soul patch.

"Hello," said Craig. His blue eyes sparkled with good humor.

Seeing him was like being hit by a second wave of the avalanche. Adam wanted to drop to his knees, throw his arms around Craig, and say, *Please, forgive me, I made a mistake, take me back!*

Only this Craig in this timeline or parallel universe or whatever didn't know who he was.

Adam needed to say *something*.

"I, um, uh, I understand you might have bought a book that I have been looking for."

"A book?"

"I'm a collector. There's a shop, in Ottawa, called *Petit Adam*, and—"

"I know that place. It's right around the corner from the Ottawa office. But I don't think I've ever been in it."

Adam blinked. Never been...?

"What's the book?" asked sweater-man.

If Adam had a ray gun he would have annihilated sweater-man where he stood.

"It's called *The Book of Regrets*. It's a curiosity, really."

Sweater-man looked at Craig, who was staring at Adam and not saying anything, and then, to fill in the silence, said, "I don't think we have anything like that."

"I've never been in that shop," said Craig. His blue eyes flashed; all friendliness was extinguished. "How did you get my name and address?"

Sweater-man looked from Craig to Adam.

Oh fuck, thought Adam. "I...I'm sorry, I must be mistaken."

"Who gave you my address?" demanded Craig.

"I think I'd better go."

The door was slammed behind him. Adam didn't waste any time driving away; he didn't want them to take down his plate number.

There was no one on the snowy road and at the corner he stopped and put the car in park. Not Craig. Someone else had bought it, a complete stranger, could be any one of a million people.

He had come here on a whim, but seeing Craig now...

Now he had regrets, and no book to write them in.

Adam stopped work on his multiverse book to scour bookshops in Quebec and Ontario and upstate New York. He put the word out that he was looking for *The Book of Regrets*. He knew it would drive up the price, but it was better to have the eyes of every bookseller in two countries looking for it than just his alone.

Finally, someone contacted him. "Interesting item," he said. "I don't have it, though. I sold it to a shop in Vermont, in Montpellier, about a month ago."

"Did you write anything in it?" asked Adam.

"No! Of course not."

The shop had sold it to a professor at the Vermont College of Fine Arts. The professor had given it as a gift to his granddaughter, who was studying English at Berkeley.

The granddaughter had loved it, but she didn't have it anymore. She didn't know where it had gone. One of her roommates had disappeared—*poof*—without a trace, like Keyser Soze. It was possible the book had been packed up with her things.

Adam tracked down the family of the missing girl.

"I'm looking for a book that may have gotten in with your daughter's things. It belonged to her roommate."

"I, oh dear, that's too bad," said the woman's faded voice on the other end of the phone. "We just, just recently, we gave all of Ally's stuff to Goodwill."

Adam wanted to bash his head against the wall. Instead he grabbed a pen and paper. "Where is this Goodwill?"

Adam called the Goodwill but they were unwilling to look for the book. He had to fly to Vancouver.

The book was not in the Goodwill shop.

So now he put the word out that there was a finder's fee. If it was ever found he might have to sell his flat to get his hands on it. Quite likely. But it wouldn't matter then, would it? He would leave all that behind.

And in this universe, this instance of the multiverse that he currently occupied, would he just disappear like the girl from Berkeley? Was that what had happened in his first life, in Cobourg in 2014? Had Craig woken up alone and spent the rest of his life wondering and grieving? It pained Adam to think so.

October 23, 2031, Santa Fe, New Mexico, USA

Adam had traded the winters of New York for a stucco house in the warmer weather of New Mexico and a comfortable nest egg to sit on during his retirement.

His multiverse book had done well. Ten years ago he had published a book on the effect of global warming on population trends, and it made a good deal of money, but as the years passed, his predictions were not realized. He was no longer prescient; the last 16 years had been new territory for him. It was time to stop and rest on his laurels.

And spend his time pursuing *The Book of Regrets*.

When his phone rang one Saturday morning, Adam made a gesture in the air that was sensed by the house AI. It was probably Marcus from the theatre group looking for a handout, or maybe his stock advisor. A ghostly virtual screen appeared in front of him, but the caller was not sharing his video feed.

"I understand you're looking for something called *The Book of Regrets*," said a middle-aged man's voice.

Adam settled back in his chair. Cranks and forgers had called before. "I am."

"I found it at an estate sale."

"The real thing?" Adam gave a dismissive chuckle. "Show me."

The video feed came on. The caller was a spare man in his forties wearing a dress shirt with the sleeves rolled to the elbows.

It was amazing, thought Adam, how much the world changed over time and men's clothing didn't.

"Here it is."

The cover filled the screen. With a twitch of his fingers in midair Adam zoomed in. There was the impression of the title in the leather.

"Show me the inside." Adam's voice shook, and he cleared his throat to cover for it.

The man paged slowly through the book. He was patient. He knew he had the real article.

"I think that's it," Adam cadged. "How much do you want for it?" He tried to sound like he didn't care all that much.

"I know you are offering a finder's fee...."

"Ten percent," said Adam firmly.

"But I got this for peanuts. 50 yuan. I want more than 5 yuan for it."

"A hundred and fifty, and I will pay for the mailing cost."

"A thousand," said the bookseller.

Anything, thought Adam. My soul! But he kept his head and scoffed. "Five hundred."

"Seven hundred."

"Four hundred."

The book was put down and the caller came into view again. Adam twitched him back to a normal zoom level, put on his best poker face, and politely shared his own video feed.

"You're supposed to go up," said the caller, "not down. That's how bargaining works."

"I offered you 500. If you are going to make me work for it, I am going to keep offering you less. If you insist on being stubborn, you will be left with a 50 yuan curiosity you can sell on EtsyBay for 50 yuan."

The man, wearing his own poker face, was silent for a minute. "I'll take the 500."

"Wise choice. Pack it carefully and overnight it."

The next day the book was in his hands, delivered to his door by UPS drone. It was the same, a little more worn, the pages a little more yellowed. Adam opened it up and reread Margaret Anne Killian's many regrets. As he progressed through the pages, though, it changed. There were new entries, and some he remembered were missing. The last one was fresh.

I regret going to Berkeley instead of going to Columbia with Keenan. I miss him!

Ally DeGuire, 2016

This was the girl who had stolen, or at least borrowed, the Book of Regrets from her roommate at Berkley. Where was she now? Had Keenan been worth it? Had she, like Adam, been unable to reconnect with her love from a past life?

Adam skimmed through but his entry was not there. He sat down at his dining room table and put the book down flat in front of him and went through every page. Twice.

Adam's entry was not there.

Adam was baffled. It looked the same, it had the same imprint of the worn-off title on the cover, and some regrets he remembered reading, even though it had been nearly sixty years. It smelled the same.

He no longer regretted not becoming a writer, because he had. Was that it? Corrected regrets disappeared and the ones remaining were still unfulfilled?

Adam took out an ordinary ballpoint, no fussing with acid-free pens this time. He hesitated with the pen above a blank sheet of paper. What if nothing happened?

What if this was not the book? What if he had just spent 500 yuan on the wrong book?

"And what if it is the right one?" he said out loud, and wrote: *I regret not meeting and marrying Craig Gellner.*

Nothing happened. Of course, he hadn't expected anything to happen yet. He went to bed and, after a lot of tossing and turning, he went to sleep.

October 25, 1972, New Liskeard, Ontario, Canada

He was ten years old again.

Adam lay in bed and felt the enormity of a life unlived pressing down on him. All those years of school, of the playground, of bullies, of memorizing pointless facts and formulas he would never use. He groaned.

"Whassamatter?" mumbled his brother beside him.

"School," groaned Adam. He was surprised again by his piping, prepubescent voice.

"Get used to it, dunderhead."

As Adam walked down the dirt road towards the school in the chill autumn morning he vowed to himself that this time he would have the career *and* the boy. Third time's the charm.

May 1, 1992, Los Angeles

Adam spent most of his third childhood and youth being impatient. He forced himself to stick with school for the sake of each diploma, which lead to the next one, which lead to his career as a journalist, which led to his career as a writer.

On his first job in New York, as a new magazine journalist, his editor opted to send him to cover the Rodney King riots in LA. He had been passed over for this assignment in his last life. It was proof to him that he was progressing, life to life, improving his skills as a journalist.

Adam booked a flight and strode boldly into what looked like a war zone with his camera, recorder, and camera bag slung across his body. He wasn't afraid. He had never been here before, but he knew the course of his life, after all. He could do whatever he wanted as long as he got himself to Toronto in July of 2008 and met Craig.

He stationed himself at the mouth of an alley, ready with his Nikon to capture the mood of the place. The rage of the oppressed. Maybe he could do something about it this time. Maybe he could write something that would have an impact so there wouldn't be a Treyvon Martin or so many others.

And then, with no warning, Adam felt a crack on the back of his head. His sight narrowed down to a pinpoint, and he fell. He didn't know why he fell, or how, only that the street came up to meet his shoulder and his side. The Nikon disappeared from his numb fingers. Sight faded in and out. There was another whack that he felt but did not hear, and consciousness left him for good.

May 2, 1972, New Liskeard, Ontario, Canada

Ten years old again. It was like getting the jail card in Monopoly: do not pass Go, do not collect $200.

Adam lay in bed immobilized. He had done it wrong. He could die; nothing was foreordained. Of course, this whole thing totally wouldn't work if it was. He had been an idiot, strutting into a war zone like that.

Adam trudged off to school, like so many other mornings. The fields weren't snowy pages waiting for him to write his marvelous life on: they were boggy with mud and spring rain, something to be slogged through—like grade five.

July 1, 2008, Toronto, Ontario, Canada
Adam had made it to the moment he met Craig at his friend Paul's Canada Day barbeque. The first time around he had very nearly not come, but car trouble had kept him in Toronto an extra day, so he decided *Why not?* This time, nothing was going to stop him from attending that barbeque.

"Adam, I'd like you to meet Craig," said Paul. Adam didn't know if this was exactly the way it had gone before. Nothing was preordained, and it made him nervous.

"Charmed," Adam put on his best smile and shook hands. He felt like a teenager on his first date.

"I've wanted to introduce you two since forever. You two could talk politics all night. Excuse me."

"Politics, eh?" said Craig. "Are you an NDP supporter?"

"Green Party." Adam smiled into Craig's blue eyes.

"Why are you looking at me like that?"

"I think you and I have a long and wonderful future together."

"Oh really?"

Adam grinned like an idiot.

Craig blinked at him. "Excuse me." He walked away.

Adam nearly swallowed his tongue. What had he done?

Adam followed Craig across the yard, but now Craig was on his phone. When he saw Adam standing there, grinning nervously, he frowned. Adam knew that frown. Craig was as sweet and polite as a petit four until you crossed a boundary.

"Can you hold for a minute?" said Craig into his phone. It was a business call. Craig was using his business voice. "Can I help you?" he asked Adam in that same voice.

"I, um, I'm sorry, we seem to have gotten off on the wrong foot." He had to fix this, only he didn't know how.

"I'm on a call."

"Let me get you a drink."

"I have a drink." Craig turned his back on Adam and went back to his call.

Adam watched Craig throughout the party. This was the time and place. This was where Craig met the man he married. If only he had a home movie of the original encounter so he could reenact it!

Craig left early and Adam followed him, only to see Craig pull away from the curb in his beat up old Volvo before Adam could catch up to him.

Adam let a few days go by. Surely things would work out. They were meant to be together. He had to try again and make a better impression this time. But when he called Paul a week later, Paul told him, "No, I may *not* give you his phone number. What did you do, Adam? He used the word *creepy*. I thought you two were just perfect for each other."

Adam tracked Craig down. He hung around outside Craig's office at lunch time. He joined the same gym. He rented a condo in Coburg and spent his weekends there milling about town, hoping to run into Craig. Deadlines were missed; his manuscript about a dystopic Trump presidency was shelved.

In January of 2010 Adam ran into Craig at a coffee shop just outside Craig's office block.

"Hello, stranger!" cried Adam cheerfully.

Craig gave Adam a flat look and said quite clearly, and loudly enough for other customers to hear, "If I just happen to run into you one more time, I am getting a restraining order."

July 12, 2014, Kingston, Ontario, Canada
Christmas Eve be damned, Adam was going to get his hands on that book as soon as it landed at *Petit Adam*. He went there every weekend and browsed. He didn't tell the bookseller, Henri, what he was looking for, but he had pretty well memorized the shelves. If there was something new in stock, he would know it.

And finally, now, he had it. Ten bucks —that was all he had paid for it. A ten-dollar gift had caused him all this trouble.

Adam leafed through. There was his touchpoint, Margaret Anne Killian's long entry. He kept going, glancing only briefly at entries that were not his own. *Brad someone. Should never have. Time is precious.*

And there it was: his own handwriting, a lifetime ago. Or was it two? *I regret not meeting and marrying Craig Gellner.* He stared at it. It was already in the book, so what was he going to do?

He went to sleep and woke up again in 2014.

Adam pondered for two days. Finally, he gathered up all the sleeping pills and codeine he could find. Los Angeles had shown him that death was the reset button. Die before you fix your regret and you start over. Things not going as planned? Go back to the beginning. As he began to float in the codeine, he wondered: was Mary Ann Killian enjoying the fountain of eternal youth by never fixing her regrets? There were so many, how could she even remember them all? Did she just keep looping through her life?

Boxing Day, 1972, New Liskeard, Ontario, Canada

Ten years old again.

Round five.

He would be more careful this time.

Christmas Day, 2014, Varadero, Cuba
"Cheers!" Craig tinked glasses with Adam and sipped his mimosa. "Mm, that's not bad."

They were sitting on the rhomboid balcony of their room and before them stretched an intensely turquoise ocean. The tops of palm trees swayed at the bottom of the view. While Craig had ferried breakfast from the room service cart to the table, Adam had unpacked the Christmas gifts. They had opened everything the night before in Coburg, except for these two items, their gifts to each other.

"Oh, this view is fantastic. I am so glad you talked me into this hotel," said Craig.

"I knew you would like it."

"Oh, the presents! So you did pack more than just your Speedo and toothbrush."

"I wore the Speedo. I packed these."

"What about the toothbrush?"

"I wore that too. Would you like to know—"

Craig shook his head. "No, I would not. Not before breakfast."

"Here, open this." Adam handed Craig an envelope.

"You got me a card?"

"Yes, just a card. Five years is paper, right?"

Craig opened the card and took out the folded piece of paper. It was a receipt from International Motors in Ottawa. Adam had blacked out all the prices.

"What is this?"

"I got the Jag restored."

"What? But, it was a write-off!"

Adam nodded. He wasn't smug. Smugness was not a thing he found he could be any more. After all his lifetimes, Adam knew that the tide of his personal history could turn at any moment. After life seven he had stopped writing his prescient books. Writing the same thing over and over was like chewing gum too long: it got flavorless and stale. Instead he puttered at this and that. Nothing was as satisfying as that first go-round as a writer, but it was the only way to keep from being bored to death lifetime after lifetime as he tried to get back together with Craig. He'd gotten close a few times, but never close enough.

Until now, life twelve.

"It won't be done for another week or two. You need the receipt to pick it up."

"Oh my God, Adam!" Craig threw his arms around Adam and kissed him till Adam struggled to get loose.

"I want to open mine!"

"Okay, here you go, I hope you like it." Little lines of worry creased Craig's brow.

"I will love it," Adam assured him.

It was an iPad Air. Adam had also stopped collecting physical books. He did not want anyone to buy him *The Book of Regrets*. He was done with it.

"No more lugging that laptop around."

"Thank you, I love it."

Craig raised his champagne flute. "Merry Christmas!"

See M.J. Gardner's story "The Book of Regrets" online at Metaphorosis.
If you liked it, leave a comment. Authors love that!
Remember to subscribe to our e-mail updates so you'll know when new stories are posted.

About the story

In writing "The Book of Regrets", I used two of my friends as the main characters. I have always used real people in creating characters, but usually just bits and pieces of them. I will take one person's habit of pursing their lips when they are thinking, another's voice, someone else's hair, facial expression, or fashion sense. Sometimes I will base minor characters on someone I know, but not that well. I had never used people I knew as themselves in a piece of writing.

This led to some problems that I hadn't anticipated. First of all, there are things I didn't know about them, or that I needed to be different to make the story work. I had to fill in the gaps, or even create them in order to fill them. I think of this as spackling.

Secondly, people are more complex than even the most nuanced fictional character. They do things that make sense—to them and to me—but would require too much backstory to explain to the reader. It's not even a question of the number of words, but of focus. It was a short story, and I didn't want too many digressions. I had to take these copies of my friends and sand them smooth.

And then there was the issue of their approval. There is a certain amount of stress involved in sending your writing out for approval, knowing that complete strangers and people you know will read it and judge you. There is more stress in sending someone a draft and saying, I used you in this, are you okay with it? (They were.) I was worried that I might offend them because no one ever sees themselves the same way someone else sees them, and the divergence in views can be jarring.

Would I do it again? Yes, if the right story came along that suited two people, as well as this one, did.

A question for the author

Q: If your writing style were a bird, what type of bird would it be and why?

A: If my writing were a bird, it would be (free-range) chicken. Chicken is a versatile food. You can smother it in slipstream, steam it with some Lovecraft, spice it up with horror and serve it with a side of suspense. You can use part or all of the chicken in dishes like BBQ short stories, novellas stuffed with cheese and mushrooms for a dinner party, or roast a whole novel for a more filling meal. No matter how you cook it, my writing is a good source of protein.

About the author

M.J. Gardner is a web developer by day, who lays in bed at night and wonders, what if....? MJ has an undergrad degree in English and Classics (Greek & Roman studies) and wrote her Master's thesis on The Vampire in English Literature. She currently lives in Windsor, Ontario, Canada with her partner of 18 years, and her cat Zoom. She is also the virtual curator of The Suicide   Museum (http://www.thesuicidemuseum.com/).

You can connect with MJ at mjgardner.com or on Twitter as @WebDivaMJ

Five Star Review

Alyssa Nabors

"We need to get serious about losing weight." my mother says as she tosses the empty pizza boxes next to the recycling bin.

"I beg your pardon?" I manage to sputter, following behind her to break the boxes down into smaller pieces that will actually fit inside the bin. My toddler, Johnny, is in bed already, but my mother insists that we have "girl time" at the end of each one of her unannounced visits.

"We all do." she says breezily. "You, me, your sister, your dad. Especially your dad!"

"Okay." I say hesitantly, hoping that this conversation will just die off if I don't engage too much.

"I mean, if you're going to have another baby, you need to be in better shape, don't you?" she takes the dishes off the table and carries them to the sink, places them on the draining board with the clean cereal bowls from this morning, with the wine glasses from last night that are waiting reproachfully to be put away.

I wait until she pours herself another glass of diet cola before I get up and rinse the dishes, leaving them in the sink for later.

My mother has, thankfully, moved on to talk about my cousin's new job, and how she'll be moving closer to the rest of the family. If you listen very carefully for the way she breathes between sentences, you can hear that my cousin is leaving her partner, and our whole family is dying to know if she'll go "back to men" when she starts dating again.

While she talks and breathes and drinks her diet cola, I stare at my reflection in the dark kitchen window and quietly hate how round my face is.

My husband Rafe comes back from walking the dog about an hour later.

He gives me a look when he sees that my mother is still here. I'm sure I have an unread text message telling me to get rid of her.

Rafe puts the dog to bed and goes into the living room. I can hear the TV go on, the recliner pop back.

"Want something to drink, babe?" I call.

Faintly, he grunts. The memory of how he used to greet me when he came home, no matter what I was doing or who was in the house, stings like antiseptic on an open wound.

My mother pauses her current monologue to cock an eyebrow at me, a smug smile passing across her face.

"A good wife wouldn't have to ask." she tells me.

I take a beer from the fridge and walk away without replying. If I speak, I might let spill the flood of vitriol I've been holding back, starting with all the things she's done and said that have driven splintering wedges into the cracks of my marriage. My face, thankfully, remains impassive.

"I'm sorry" I whisper as I hand Rafe the bottle. "She'll be gone soon, I swear."

He doesn't look at me. He grunts again.

I see — or rather shove — my mother to the door, and find Rafe lying in bed staring at his phone.

"I'm sorry." I say again, lamely.

"I'm not gonna tell you your mom can't come to our house." he says flatly, not taking his eyes off of the screen. The argument is so old that it sits like an invalid dementia patient in the corner — nearly irrelevant, but not dead yet. Inside, I imagine what it would be like if he looked me in the eye and said what he really felt, what he really thought. If he would just tell me how to fix the broken bridge separating us from each other.

I sigh, undressing and carefully placing my dirty clothes and the ones he has discarded on the floor and the back of the chair in the corner in the hamper.

"Did you hear what she said about dieting?" I ask, closing my eyes wearily, as I run a hairbrush through my messy curls.

Rafe makes a half-hearted jerk of the head and torso that could be interpreted by the generous as a sympathetic shrug. Standing there topless at the end of the bed, hair loose around my shoulders, I give him a shy smile.

"I mean, I'm not so bad, right?"

He looks me in the face then, his eyes startlingly focused.

"You're the one that keeps letting her tear you down like this, I don't know how you can expect me to rebuild your self-esteem every time Momzilla comes tearing through."

I turn away abruptly, going to the dresser and hurriedly throwing on an old pair of flannel pajama pants and an oversized t-shirt. Rafe sighs, and the bed springs groan as he gets up, tossing his phone on the nightstand with a soft clatter.

He stands behind me as I finish dressing, just within arms' reach. I want him to close that gap so badly, to wrap himself around me and tell me that everything is fine, really. For a moment, I think that he might go as far as to stroke my hair, or take my hand.

"I'm sorry," he mutters, "of course you're beautiful. You're wonderful. I love you."

His voice sounds nearly ashamed, as if saying those things costs him something. His honesty?

"It's fine." I say, in an overly bright voice. "You've had a long day, and I know —"

I know you hate my mother? I know you aren't attracted to me anymore? I know you wish we weren't behind on the mortgage and that the shower weren't clogged and that the dog would stop peeing on the welcome mat, and that somehow you've decided all these things are my fault?

"I'm doing my best," Rafe says quietly, almost defensively, then in a softer tone, "we both are, right? We're doing the best we can with what we've got."

Another memory slithers into my mind, fangs dripping with venom. A younger, thinner me and a smiling, warm Rafe. The tiny apartment that didn't heat properly and flooded easily, and the way we laughed huddling together under a pile of thrift-store quilts, the way we synchronized when damming the leaky floorboards against the third day of a rainstorm.

"Yeah..." my voice trails off, unconvincing and barely present.

Rafe retreats, falling onto the bed, holding the phone in front of his face like a shield.

I sit on the couch with my laptop. There's a mostly-empty package of Oreos next to me; it was full when I started. I told Rafe I had to finish something for work when I put my pajamas on, but I've just been window-shopping on a half-dozen or so websites. Retail therapy by proxy. Not that my actual work isn't demanding my attention, but... I admit to myself that work is the one place where I can put my own needs before everyone else's demands.

It's nearly midnight when I click an ad by accident. For a second I'm positive I just downloaded a virus because in no way can it be a serious ad.

CLOSEOUT SALE — DISPOSABLE TIME MACHINES

I'm relieved and slightly incredulous when I'm not suddenly faced with a million pop up ads, but only redirected to a listing on a popular e-commerce site.

There's no picture, but the product description is pretty unbelievable:

Portable time displacement device, good for revisiting one moment on your personal timeline, return trip to present included. For use of one person only. Warning: residual memories of alternate timelines are probable after-effects of product use. Biodegradable, 100% eco-friendly.

I snort, blowing chocolate crumbs all over my keyboard.

I scroll down to read the reviews, expecting either gullible idiots with disappointed hopes or trolls who fancy themselves in on the joke.

[Verified Purchaser] The Disposable Time Machine allowed me to go back and tell my past self not to start a relationship with the man that cheated on me. 5 Stars.

Ugh. Trolls with really bad taste, apparently.

[Verified Purchaser] I was skeptical, but this machine actually allowed me to say goodbye to my father before his fatal heart attack. However, my past self was not able to persuade him to go to a hospital

preventing his death altogether which was my original goal. 3 Stars.

Jesus.

[Anonymous] I used this machine to go back and allow my little brother to drown in the pool when we were kids. If he had lived, he would have been diagnosed with inoperable stage 4 pancreatic cancer a year later. My mother would have ruined her health caring for him and none of my siblings or I would be able to afford college. No rating given.

I close the laptop for a second, feeling sick.

I close my eyes and try to breathe deeply, try to let my mind clear.

There's a small part of me that wonders what part of my history I could change. If Rafe had taken that job. If I hadn't been in that accident. If Rafe had been able to get that scholarship. If we had never met because I was confident enough to take that study abroad course... If, if, if.

I open the laptop again. I stare at the screen.

I let the mouse hover over "Add to Cart", an unbearable tease that goes on for a long, silent moment. I picture some version of myself that knows about fashion and flies to New York for business and has never worried about having a second chin. Or a third miscarriage. I picture someone who doesn't clean up after everyone, who has a spine like polished steel and comes home from work feeling like she accomplished something bigger than staving off foreclosure for another month.

As though by divine appointment, Rafe lets out a eardrum-rupturing snore at the same time that Johnny wakes with a startled cry.

I close the laptop, hurrying to bring my son water and quiet him before his father wakes.

When he's been sufficiently calmed and kissed, I go back to the couch, carefully brush all the cookie crumbs into my hand, and dump them into the wastebasket on my way to bed.

The next day I bring Johnny to my parents' house. My mother is out, shopping with my sister. My dad makes pancakes in weird shapes, sprinkling in chocolate chips, alternating making silly faces and monkey noises at Johnny. Anything to make him grin in his little booster seat, where he sits stuffing blueberries and banana slices in his face.

I'm sipping a cup of coffee — mostly milk, actually, my dad likes his roast so dark you need a flashlight — and my mind keeps wandering back to the weird ad from the night before. I know it had to be one of the April Fool's pages that never got taken down. But I can't help but leaf through the pages of my own life, wondering what edits I would make if I had the chance.

"Hey Dad," I ask absently, reaching for the can of whipped cream to pile more whipped cream onto my pancakes, "if you could change something in your past, what would it be?"

Dad blows a raspberry at Johnny and looks back at me, his head cocked at a strange angle.

"I dunno, babe." he says slowly. "I guess I'm pretty happy with the way things are right now. Do you want a little more coffee?"

I nod. He lifts the old pot from its ancient burner and pours a bit into my mug. He brings the milk jug from the fridge, a thoughtful look still on his face.

"I guess I could always go back and tell myself about some big stock market thing, or all the Super Bowl winners or something? Take you guys on a nice vacation or help you pay off more of your student loans."

"There's nothing you would do for yourself?" I ask without thinking, still off in my own world. He shakes his head.

"What do I need?" he shrugs, looking fondly at me, and over at Johnny who is determinedly reaching for an open bottle of maple syrup. "As long as you all are happy, that's enough for me."

I put the maple syrup out of Johnny's reach. He squawks in wordless indignation, but Grandpa is there in the nick of time to distract with a bite of pancake. I look at the two of them fondly as they smile at each other, one face smeared with chocolate, the other dusted with flour. But as my mind aimlessly wanders through all the might-have-beens it can summon, my eyes lose focus. I don't see them anymore.

I see that person that Rafe still runs to kiss after he walks in the door. I see someone who doesn't dread holidays because they inevitably involve someone storming out or locking themselves in the bathroom, crying hysterically. I see someone who doesn't have to think about her husband or her child and is free to go off and find all the different potential versions of herself, picking and choosing parts until she Frankensteins together the perfect life.

"What if I'm not happy?" I say softly to myself.

Johnny is pulling Dad's reading glasses off his head, so Dad doesn't hear.

After Johnny is in bed, and Rafe is asleep, I go back to read more reviews. The page isn't hard to find — I don't even have to use my internet history. It's the first thing that comes up when I search for "personal time machine".

I comb through the reviews, looking for a skeptic or a dissatisfied customer, or even a link to Snopes or some other site to debunk the whole thing. Before I know it, I'm at the end. Down in the company contact information, I spot something interesting.

Still on the fence? Try our one-time-only free sample via company associate!

What did that mean? I'm too curious now to resist clicking the link.

A chat window opens.

Megan: Hello, how can I help you this evening?

Cust19423: Hi, what is the free sample?

Megan: The free sample is a small-scale reusable device that one of our company associates can use to show you the effectiveness of this line of products. I'd be happy to offer you a demonstration if you have the time to answer a few quick questions?

Cust19423: Um, sure.

Megan: Ok, great! Please confirm that the following information is correct:

The next message contains my full name, date of birth, address, Rafe's full name, Jonny's full name, my place of employment, and my current job title. I have to stifle a shriek, and begin typing furiously.

Cust19423: WHAT THE HELL?! How do you have all my information??? How do you know all that??

Did you hack my computer? Do you have my SSN too???

Megan: Please remain calm, ma'am. When you clicked on the offer of free sample, you did agree to disclose some personal information, but I assure you our system is completely secure.

Cust19423: This seems really shady.

Megan: If you would like to discontinue the free sample, you can disconnect at any time. Would you like to stop?

Cust19423: No… I want to keep going.

Megan: I'm happy to help you with that. Can you please choose from one of the following options:

(A) Diet

(B) Finance

(C) Education

Cust19423: What is this for?

Megan: I will be making a minor, completely positive adjustment to your timeline in one of these three categories. Please choose one.

Cust19423: A, I guess. Diet.

Megan: That sounds great. Please wait one moment.

Megan: We hope that you have enjoyed your free sample and that you will consider purchasing one of our full products or experiences before the closeout sale ends! Have a great night!

The chat window closes.

"I didn't screenshot anything!" I groan to myself. "No one at the police station will believe me, and without a police report, none of the credit agencies will take this seriously either."

I let my head fall back against the couch.

After a few deep breaths, I set my laptop aside and go to my secret stash of snacks in the kitchen. There are a few Oreos left, I know... but they're gone. I mutter to myself, wondering if Rafe got to them. Then I notice that next to the pantry, the recycling is empty. No pizza boxes.

I whip my phone out and scroll through the pictures. There's Johnny eating pancakes but the picture of my perfect plate... gone. I freeze. I slowly run my hands over my stomach, my thighs, my chin. I *feel* different.

I run back to the laptop. My credit card is in my hand faster than I thought possible. I pay extra for overnight shipping. I leave a really nice review for Megan.

I can't stop staring at myself in the mirror the next morning. I run to the bathroom at work at least a dozen times, unable to believe the way my clothes fit, *actually* fit my body. It feels like everyone is smiling at me, everyone is complimenting me. This is how they treat me even though as far as they know, I've always looked like this.

I can't stop the excitement building in me — Rafe left for work before my alarm went off, swapping to the early shift as he does every few months. He'll already be there when I get home. I call my dad and arrange for him to get Johnny from daycare — surprise date night, I say. Dad sounds surprised, but happily agrees. I float through the rest of the day, giddy with the memories of the candlelit dinners of our first year in our first apartment. And then, I think to myself, when Rafe goes to pick up Johnny, I'll cancel that order. I don't need anything else.

When I get home, I almost dance through the door.

"Hello," I call out in my most seductive voice, "anybody home?"

Rafe makes some unintelligible response from the recliner.

"Hi, you." I lean over him and kiss the tip of his nose.

"Hey." he says, seeming slightly perturbed, "Where's Johnny?"

"With Dad," I say breezily, "I thought it would be nice to have dinner out, just the two of us."

Rafe lets out a surprised, incredulous laugh.

"Out? With what money?" his face looks darker somehow, "We can't afford 'out' right now, or did you somehow forget that?"

"I'm not talking about some five-star restaurant here," I said defensively, my mood quickly spoiling, "I just thought—"

"You didn't think, though!" Rafe gets up from his chair, disgusted, "You never think about the big picture, it's always a mani-pedi here, and a new toy for Johnny there, and you just don't process how these things add up!"

"God, Rafe, you act like a date night with your wife is going to get us evicted or something!" I wrap my arms around myself, face burning red.

"Well maybe if you gave me a heads up when you go off on one of these impulsive tears, I'd actually have some input into what was happening in my own life!" he snapped, snatching the dog's leash from its hook by the door and storming out. Without the dog.

I stand frozen for a minute, my eyes brimming with hot, angry tears. My phone dings, and I scrub at my eyes with the back of my hands.

It's a picture of Johnny and my mom. Johnny's wearing a new shirt that says, "Mimi said I could," his cheek sporting a red lipstick smear.

Another ding.

"Good luck with your little date night."

"Didn't work out. Coming to get Johnny." I text back.

"Oh well," comes the reply, "A good wife knows when to surprise, and when to plan ahead."

I grip the phone so tightly my knuckles turn white.

It dings again.

"Package will be delivered tomorrow, 9:30 a.m."

While I wait for my order to arrive, Johnny sits in my lap, playing with a plastic dinosaur I don't remember buying for him. He says we bought it at the grocery store. Rafe didn't come home before I fell asleep, and left before I woke up.

My dad wasn't there when I picked up Johnny, just my mother, smiling that Cheshire Cat grin. Apparently, there was a very important errand she needed him to run, and a good husband does whatever their wife needs them to.

Johnny's soft curls tickle my chin as he sings to himself. He smells like soap and the sticky sweetness of fruit. I close my eyes and savor the warmth of his small body leaning against my chest, the sound of his voice.

When the doorbell rings I put Johnny on the floor and he fusses.

I sign for the package and take it quickly, shutting the door behind me. I strew styrofoam and leaflets of instructions in different languages all over the kitchen counters. It assembles so quickly, so easily. Like a pocket radio, almost.

Johnny tugs at my pant leg. I look down at him, frozen. The events of the last few days fly like a blur through my minds' eye. My only son relegated to a background figure in the most important decision in my life. The weight of the machine in my hand and the pull of his small hands are both agony.

I take a deep breath.

I kiss the top of his head.

"Mommy's not going anywhere." I lie.

I turn the dial.

See Alyssa N. Vaughn's story "Five Star Review" online at Metaphorosis.
If you liked it, leave a comment. Authors love that!
Remember to subscribe to our e-mail updates so you'll know when new stories are posted.

About the story

Part of this story came from my annual fury with ThinkGeek for offering products that aren't real every April Fools' Day. I wanted to imagine a scenario where they were offering a product that sounded fake but was actually ready to ship, 100% functional. But instead of thinking about what chaos would happen when ThinkGeek started selling time machines and all the temporal paradox stuff that would go with it, I got really stuck on what a person would have to go through to actually travel through time with the intention of changing something about their past.

A question for the author

Q: Duckbilled platypus – result of divine distraction, or alternate universe crossover?

A: So the platypus belongs to the mammalian subclass Prototheria, which sounds like a kingdom from World of Warcraft and most of the animals that belong to that group are extinct. It's pretty much the platypus and the echidna, and both of them are weird as crap. Did you know that the echidna doesn't have nipples? It has milk patches on its skin instead. So does the platypus. And the platypus is one of the only venomous mammals. It only produces its venom during the platypus mating season. What the heck?

Honestly, my favorite thing about the platypus is that it is one of several species that have hypothetically stopped evolving. They said "yup, being a venomous beaver-duck is totally working for me, y'all go on ahead" and that's how we got platypi. They are nature's old man, grumbling about these species today, with their placentas and their nipples and their non-beak-faces and their no-venom-producing-claws. The platypus wants you to stop trying to explain Snapchat to it and go outside once in a while, for goodness sake.

I may be a platypus.

I'm really stuck on the subclass though. "Your quest will take you to Prototheria, therein you must seek the strange creature of venomous claw and hideous beak, very nearly the last of its kind…"

About the author

Alyssa N. Vaughn was born and raised somewhere between Dallas and Fort-Worth, Texas, and she now lives very *very* near the house where she grew up, with her husband, children, and dogs, only very narrowly missing an "Everybody Loves Raymond" situation. She has been a public radio employee, a software developer, a high school teacher, and an assistant director at a computer camp. She was a writer before, during, after, and about each of these professions.

blog.anvaughn.com, @msalyssaenvy

Two Villains, a Notebook, and a Lump of Coal

Helen French

Alone in a badly-lit corridor in the still of night, Leora wondered if she'd made a terrible mistake.

She'd stolen what she'd broken into Namose College to steal and yet it felt like everything was on the verge of going wrong.

Nothing good had ever happened to her in this vile magician's den, that was true. But she was halfway out of the building. Victory, of a sort, was hers.

And yet… There was something wrong with the air. It didn't smell right.

She carried on towards the way out. Now and then she stopped, sure she'd heard a noise, that someone would discover her trespassing at any moment.

Eventually, she came to a set of doors that were not her exit but instead an entrance to the stairwell, leading both up to the higher floors of the college, and down into the basement. Tendrils of smoke crept out from underneath the doors.

She pushed one open out of curiosity, only to find another person on the other side of it, slowly coming up the stairs.

They both paused.

The man opposite looked like a student, who ought to know in an instant that she was a fraud and sound the alarm for intruders...

But, she noticed, his robes were much like hers. Mistakes where there should be smoothness. Bad stitching where it should be seamless. He didn't belong either.

Yet if he too were a fraud, he was playing a different game to her. Behind him, heavy smoke was curling slowly to the ceiling. He grasped blackened rods in his hands.

He'd started a fire? If he'd discovered one, he certainly wasn't raising a warning. Leora stared at him for another beat of her heart, maybe five, then he shrugged at her and carried on going up the staircase. Leora didn't feel inclined to follow. What he was doing wasn't any of her business as long she could get out of there safely.

Once she was out, Leora stood in the park across from Namose as the fire spread, unable to tear her gaze away.

The college was an ugly building that burned even uglier. It had been born a single white tower, glorious in its simplicity, then ruined with countless extensions – one made of glass, another of red brick, another of wood, and so on.

Now set alight, smoke and ash smeared itself onto every surface it could find. The facade was beginning to crumble.

Leora liked to think its ugliness came from the inside, that it could've been beautiful if different people had lived inside it.

A crowd of inquisitive bystanders emerged around her as the fire grew larger. They oohed and ahhed with each new explosion or burst of flames as if they were watching fireworks.

"All those poor, uppity conjurers without a home," said a reedy voice to the side of her. Martin 'Ose, her oldest friend – only friend – had arrived.

"A real tragedy," Leora replied, watching carefully as a corner of the glass conservatory collapsed. "But it's nice to see you. Fire bring you out?"

"Brought everyone out," Martin said. He turned to her with a grin. "Do I sense your touch anywhere in this business?" He gestured to the flames, out of control, high above the white tower.

"Don't be indiscreet," she said, pushing his hand down. "And stop grinning. Before you say anything, that doesn't mean it's anything to do with me. Maybe if I'd come up with the idea…"

"Do you think many will die?"

"I hope the worst ones do," she replied, even as she could see dozens of them escaping, climbing out of every door and window available. "I'd quite happily bury them in one of those giant holes they pull all their magic out of."

She'd nearly fallen in one once, ten years ago.

She'd been a mere ten years old, and as a birthday present her father had dragged her to the Namose hole for testing, thinking success might bring them fortune.

At twenty feet across and at least twenty feet deep, it looked like a sinkhole, but human hands had made it, widening it year by year as more and more Namosians leant into it for extra power. It was carved out of the ground around the back of the college, in the middle of a large clearing surrounded by trees.

On testing day, ten magicians waited by the side of the crater, dispassionate expressions on their faces, as child after child tried to call magic from the earth.

Most failed. One – Gally Karness, whom Leora vaguely remembered fighting with when they were little – whooped with joy when she somehow created a temporary waterfall inside the hole.

When it was her turn, Leora lay down on the ground and put her arm over the edge of the hole. She pressed her palm flat against the earth as she'd been told and mentally tried to pull something from the soil. Nothing happened.

Leora didn't know what to do. Her father would say she'd let her mother down; a common accusation whenever he wanted to hurt her. Mother was long dead, but Leora still missed her.

"Time to move," one of the magicians ordered.

Don't rush her," said another, a tall woman with long hair. "There's something about this one, I'm sure."

"Perhaps, Halve," the first shrugged, "but if she had earth magic we'd have seen it by now."

"Please," Leora asked, from her awkward position on the ground.

"One more try," said Halve grudgingly. "But don't let us down."

This time Leora decided to flat-out cheat.

She leant over as far as she could, so they wouldn't see, and instead of pressing her palm against the wall of the earth, she held it close but not quite touching. Ever since she was little Leora had been able to feel the magic of the air. As she grew older, it was as easy as breathing to cream some off the top. All she had to do was hold her hand still as could be, feel the energy, then draw it in.

What she could do best was finding things. Could be something lost, could be something she needed. She'd never found riches just by thinking about it, but the neighbors knew her well enough to pay a little coin now and then if there was something small they wanted looking for. Lockets, lost animals, a stash of liquor perhaps – the magic led her to them.

She focused on finding something new or big that might impress these judging magicians. Then, letting the air magic guide her, she felt something. It tickled her palm at first... something rough, something sticking out of the earth that hadn't been there before. She stuck her tongue out as she pulled hard, then stood up triumphant, holding her treasure in the air.

Only to look up and see she'd found a lump of coal.

All the magicians laughed at her, except for Halve, who looked furious.

Her father rushed over and started trying to usher her away but Halve walked around the edge of the hole to meet them. She held out her hand and grabbed the edges of the blackened chunk. "Something we can remember you by," she said loudly. "You embarrassed me," she said in a quieter voice. "I don't want to see you here again."

Leora didn't want to give the coal up. She held on tight. Her father wrested it away, his hands callused and hot. Then he gave it to the magician like it was nothing. "You've shamed us all," he whispered on the long walk home. "What would your mother say?"

Leora didn't go back to Namose until five years later.

The evening had begun with her father throwing his mug of beer across the room. "You're good at finding things. Go find some money!"

Leora wiped the edges of her skirt where some of the liquid had spilled. "You know it's not that simple."

"Rent's due," he said, shrugging. "We won't make it unless you do something."

She swore softly. He spent all his coin on beer. Leora struggled to earn any at all unless it was through finding things for people, and they too expected more than she could offer. Granny's misplaced necklace – fine. Expensive jewels that they wanted but had never owned – well it hadn't happened yet, had it?

She wished she could leave him to it, but the only good memories she had were at home, back when mother was alive, back when home meant comfort and happiness. At least he'd stuck around when the worst happened. Other men might've gone years ago.

She kicked an empty chair – her father didn't blink an eye – and stormed out of the house. They lived on a narrow road on the edge of Critan, where the houses were cramped and small, for families whose parents had employment but not much of it. No one had work for her – she'd asked all of them the day before – and she couldn't steal from them. Not if she wanted to keep on living around there.

She walked for an age, ending up at the biggest building in the city: Namose College. She knocked until somebody pulled open a little hole in the door.

"No more deliveries today," a voice said.

"Not a delivery, though I could do that if you wanted. I'm looking for employment."

The door opened. It was Halve behind it, the magician who'd tested her all those years ago. "Let's talk in my office," she said.

"The truth is, we don't really have work for outsiders," she said from behind a dark wooden desk, in a spacious room lined with bookshelves. Leora tried not to marvel at the fineness of it all. "The people here study exceedingly hard to protect this country. We are not here to offer work to the neighbors. *We* are already working for *you*."

Leora stopped listening once it became clear Halve had invited her in for a lecture and nothing more. On the shelves behind her, amongst all the books on history and earth power, sat a solid black lump with a rough, choppy surface.

It didn't matter what you discovered if you couldn't take it. Leora's fingers itched. "I think I found that coal," she said, pointing at it, trying to sound as if it meant nothing to her at all. And really it shouldn't have done. "I was a child," she said, "here for the testing a long time ago."

The magician laughed, leaning back in her chair. "I remember you. Think many children give us coal instead of magic? I keep it as a symbol of what people will cling to."

"I found it," Leora heard herself saying, almost like the words had thrown themselves out of her mouth. "It's mine and I'd like it back."

Halve stood up. "I'm afraid it's time for you to leave."

She rounded the desk and grabbed Leora's arm to pull her to the door.

"Gally!" she called into the corridor.

As she was being dragged, Leora – now fueled by fury – stole the only thing in grabbing distance, a small notebook on the side of the desk, and shoved it up her top. She could figure out later whether it was worth anything.

Gally led her back out. "Funny world isn't it," she said, smiling lightly. "Born two streets apart, and I get to live in Namose while you aren't even allowed to beg here."

Leora snarled at her. "Funny? You breeze around, funded by the Kingdom, while your old friends struggle for their next meal. You think I care about you and me when there's a whole world of difference between us?"

Gally pushed the door open. "There's a world of difference because we're employed to save you people. We have to be better than you. I'm not sorry about that."

"Are you sorry for being a dick?" Leora asked, then grinned as Gally raised her fists.

Leora had been in significantly more fights than Gally, so the tussle was one-sided to begin with. After a few quick jabs she knocked Gally into the door, where she hit her mouth hard on the doorknob and fell to the ground.

Gally looked up from where she lay, blood dripping from her mouth, and smiled.

Leora realized her mistake too late.

Lying fully on the earth, Gally wouldn't need to dig a hole to draw power from it.

Gally pushed herself up to kneeling, muttering magic as she went. Her hands clawed down and soil spat up.

Leora went to run at her but something invisible punched her hard in the side. Before she could react, another thud landed hard on her shoulder, knocking her to her knees.

Then some kid jumped between them. Thin. Smaller than her. Unsteady on his feet. "Leave her alone," he yelled.

As if Gally were going to pay attention to a brat like him. Leora sighed. She was going to get her arse kicked.

But Gally stopped. "You," she said with a disdainful sneer. Then Gally looked around the boy to point at Leora. "Don't come back."

She disappeared with a slam of the college doors.

The boy wandered over to Leora and held a hand out, though he didn't look strong enough to pull her up. Leora leaned on him anyway. "Thanks," she said, not used to feeling grateful.

"I'm Martin," he replied. "Anyone they hate, I like."

And with those few words, Leora liked him back. "Want to see a notebook I found?"

Leora laughed to herself as the flames burned on.

"What's going on in that head of yours?" Martin asked.

"Memories, that's all. Thinking about when you had to rescue me from a fight right over there. The day we met. I'd never seen anything so ridiculous."

"I had no choice," Martin replied, in a mocking tone. "I pitied the poor girl being beaten by the magician and had to intervene. Good thing she was so afraid of me."

"Afraid? It was your name she didn't like, nothing else."

"The joys of being an 'Ose."

Leora felt for him. Very few magicians kept their children. They were given the name 'Ose and fostered out instead.

They fell to silence for a short while, watching the flames blaze.

"Your mother could be dead in there," Leora said to Martin, as if that fact might comfort him somehow.

He shrugged at the smoke and the darkness. "I still don't know who she is. For all I know, she deserves it."

"Ever imagine what life might've been like if she'd kept you?"

"Can't imagine any world where a magician would keep someone like me." He meant his legs, which weren't very strong. Something to do with his birth taking too long. Or at least that's how it had been explained to him. "It doesn't matter. I prefer reality."

Leora reached out and squeezed his hand. "Let's stay in it, then."

But her mind wandered. Thinking about Martin's mother led to thinking about her father, which inevitably led to thinking about his final days.

One year ago, nineteen-year-old Leora had spent an evening writing notes among the ever-decreasing margins in the stolen notebook.

She finished marking the new prices they'd have to pass down to the retailers, and went to blow the candle out when she heard a thud behind her.

A hand clasped over her mouth, hot breath on her ear. Then a voice. "You're coming with us. Don't scream. It'll only make things worse." Dread and certainty settled in Leora's stomach. She'd always known this day would come. Rip off enough traders and sooner or later one will come looking for you.

Not seeing a way out of it, she let herself be led into the cool outside air.

The man was rough and his friends, who emerged so suddenly it was as if they were made out of the night, more so. They pushed her down the street, and when Leora caught sight of her drunken father stumbling down an alleyway and casting a confused look in her direction, she hoped to the earth's core that he saw her shaking her head. *Don't follow me. Go home. Be your usual obnoxious self there.*

She was relieved to see him sit down, his back against the wall of the alleyway, drinking whatever he had in his flask. With luck he'd stay there until morning.

A mile or so later, she was pushed into a storeroom. Its shelves were full and the white floor under their feet was cleaned and polished. This was a building of some wealth.

Of the men who'd accosted her, one waited at her side while the other two went back outside. They ignored her pleas for information.

An age later a small man with a smug, round face appeared from a door on the other side of the storeroom. "Did you get it?"

Her attacker passed over an object: The notebook. The recipe book.

Leora's stomach started to freefall. Shit and damnation. Martin would be furious. All that work gone.

And then she realized. She had to be inside the storerooms around the back of Namose. The shelves all around her... she almost smiled. She'd made a fortune out of all those jars.

The small man pursed his lips as he flicked through the book. The recipes were half-spells. Not the actual components of magic, but things to improve it. Powder for their hands to increase the power they pulled from the earth. A drink that could increase how long their magic might last. All featured strange ingredients.

"When did you work out what to do with this?" he asked.

Leora shrugged. "I don't know what you're talking about."

The man sighed. "It took us a long time to realize what was going on. Price-gouging every single unique material we needed. Buying up stocks so that our retailers only had a few places to go to. Increasing the prices bit by bit."

"Sounds like natural price variances," she said.

"Our funds to strengthen this country, frittered away."

"Wasn't me," she said stubbornly.

"We think it was. A little girl with big aspirations."

That angered her. "I'm a grown woman, damn it," she began, but she couldn't answer the rest of the question because just then there was a commotion at the door. It opened and a man with a familiar face fell to his knees on the floor.

No, no, no. Leora knelt next to her father. "What are you doing here?"

But she knew. For the first time in his life he'd found himself curious about what Leora was up to and he couldn't have picked a worse time to do it.

The small man looked cheered. "Ah, the convenient arrival of your father means we don't need to threaten anyone else you care about."

Leora stood up. "You don't have to threaten anyone."

"Don't I? You've been stealing our money for four years."

"I won't do it anymore," she said. Better to promise her future away than wait until they involved Martin, too. They worked together, of course. Leora found the goods and the contacts to sell them, and Martin was the brains behind their pricing strategy.

One of the thugs from outside brought in a large water collector. Full to the brim, it dripped murky water onto the clean floor.

Leora stepped forward. "What if I tell you whatever it is you want to know?"

"This is a punishment, not torture for information."

Then it began. Dunking her father in until he couldn't breathe, until he vomited when they did bring him out for a brief respite, only to submerge him again.

Leora wept. "Can't you use magic instead?" she begged, trying to think of anything at all that wouldn't be so cruel. She tried to use her own magic to find a weapon on the shelves behind her, but she couldn't keep her head cool enough to focus.

"No. It would be a waste of our powers."

The punishment continued, until her father was half-unconscious and Leora's throat raw from crying.

"Next time we'll burn you alive," the small man said.

He threw her out the door, and her father with her.

They stumbled home in the darkness.

But the next morning her father did not wake up and go out in search of wine or beer. He did not sit at the kitchen table complaining or telling her to make money.

Leora looked for him when the quiet became too much, and found him in bed in the same position she'd left him in, his face grey and his body cold.

Her poor, awful father. Gone forever. The magicians almost certainly to blame, but nothing she could do about it. Nothing she could even think of to do to them.

She hated them all.

That hatred had never ebbed, not even twelve long months later. It had propelled her into the college that night, looking to take what was hers.

That someone had sought to burn the place down at the same time was a bonus.

Most of the crowd had faded away as the night wore on, as the magicians' attempts failed, as the building continued to burn, but there were still enough bystanders for Leora and Martin to stand among them unnoticed.

"You honestly had nothing to do with this?" Martin asked, trying his luck one more time.

Leora shook her head. "No – honestly. I was in there, all right, but I didn't start it. I had other plans. Sometimes there's more than one villain at work at any time."

"You wanted the notebook back," he stated.

"No. It's not important any more. Maybe if I'd got there earlier I'd have done a finding, but there wasn't time. As long as it burns up with the rest of the place I'll be happy."

Leora opened up a large pocket on the side of her coat and showed Martin what was inside.

"Coal?" he asked. "Your coal?"

"Yesterday was the anniversary of father dying and I didn't think I cared 'til it came. Once I stopped crying, I decided I wanted a small piece of revenge.

"This is what I went in for. Halve had this on a shelf in her room all these years."

"Scum," Martin said, then spat at the ground.

"Indeed."

"Sometimes I think we'd be better off away from this place, burnt down or not. It's no good for either of us living here."

Leora exhaled loudly. "If it were that easy to start over somewhere new, I'd have gone years ago."

They stood side by side until the fire was only a glow. Martin waited for Leora's nod and shuffled home. Leora left in the opposite direction, striding away full of thought and satisfaction.

The next morning, after a negligible amount of sleep, Leora waited by the pond on the edge of the city. She'd chosen the location for its proximity to Martin's house, to ease his journey ahead of what might turn into a very long day.

He was sniffing at the air when he finally approached. "That fire still stinks."

"Still burning, most likely."

He stubbed his toe into the ground, turning the grass over. "Gonna tell me why we're here?"

Leora pulled her prize out of her pocket once more.

"This again?"

"It's not coal," she said to his questioning look. "It was *never* coal."

"That makes no sense whatsoever."

"I assumed it was coal, but I was ten years old, wasn't I? Halve stole it off me and put it on a shelf. No one's ever seriously looked at this thing. We all assumed its insides matched its outsides, that it was nothing important."

"Yes," he said slowly.

"But you and I should know better than that. Assuming *anything* is dangerous. I found this in a magic hole, for earth's sake. For all I know, it was buried there long ago by the very first Namose magicians. Perhaps the sheer desperation I felt as a child, failing my tests, led me to it."

Martin shrugged. "Still doesn't look like anything special."

Leora turned it over. The other side was a mess where she'd spent half the morning taking it apart. Inside, something glistened. "The more I held it, the warmer it got. The warmer it got, the softer and waxier it got. When I started picking at it, the layers peeled away." Leora dug her fingers in, wrestled around, and pulled out a stone. It was largely dull but shone in one corner.

"Is that a diamond?" Martin asked in wonder.

"I think so," Leora said. "Not the only one, either." Her hand closed around it and she shoved it in her pocket again. "It's worth a small fortune. They probably won't even know it's missing, considering the fire. But I'm not staying here. The building's gone but those bastards will rebuild. These diamonds could take me across the world. Only thing is, I don't want to do it on my own. Will you come too?"

"Do you really have to ask?"

They packed up that afternoon, just in case anyone had seen Leora at the College and might come looking for her.

It began to pour down as they walked out of the city, but the raindrops fell too late to soothe Namose's smoldering ruins.

Leora scowled at its remains as they strolled past. She shifted the bag she carried on her shoulder, and hoped they could get away quickly.

There was only one moment for pause on their journey, when they came to a crossroads and saw a figure on the other side, most likely waiting for a horse or carriage. Leora thought she recognized the man, that he was the firestarter she'd encountered in Namose. He too had a heavy bag, as if he'd had to run from something.

She didn't want to ask outright and arouse suspicion if it wasn't him, but she couldn't say nothing, either. So instead she simply waved.

The man waved back, and Leora couldn't resist. "Thank you!" she yelled.

"You're welcome," he shouted as reply.

"I think he looked a bit like you," Leora said to Martin later, as they walked further into the countryside. It would take a good few nights of camping before they'd find a town in which to sell their merchandise. "A cousin perhaps."

"Even a brother," Martin suggested. "I wouldn't know. They foster us out to so many different places."

"So many children," Leora said with a sigh. "So many left hungry for something more out of life."

"And of the two you know," Martin said with a grin, "one's most likely burned down a building to make himself feel better about it all, and the other's run off to see the world with a diamond thief. It's not all bad."

No, it wasn't, she supposed, letting herself smile for once. Smiling was hard. So was hope – but she thought she could get better at both with time, now that they finally seemed worthwhile.

With every step they took away from Critan and Namose, she felt lighter, as if a pressure she hadn't realised was on her were finally melting away.

She decided that she'd never look back.

The past was ashes and ruin. The future could be almost anything at all.

See Helen French's story "Two Villains, a Notebook, and a Lump of Coal" online at Metaphorosis.
If you liked it, leave a comment. Authors love that!
Remember to subscribe to our e-mail updates so you'll know when new stories are posted.

About the story

The very basic origin of this story is rather straightforward- it was the phrase 'Fired up' as a story prompt for a writers group that I'm in. It's fascinating to see how people can interpret the same prompt in so many different ways.

I decided to go with a character fired up with anger, and a literal fire. A fantasy world came into life from there: a magician's college burning down. Then the main character Leora popped into my head – angry at everything, and happy to see a building on fire and lives at risk.

Why? I knew she'd have a sympathetic story to tell, and that we'd see bits of it leak out gradually, revealing how she came to be inside the building just before it caught fire, and why she's so unapologetic about her part in it.

However, I didn't want to write a story that was all darkness and no light. I enjoy friendships in fiction, so I added in her best friend Martin and a relationship that was truly solid and platonic. These are two people who have been through a lot and would do anything for one another.

The hardest bit was incorporating flashbacks in a natural way. Leora had three significant moments in her life that led her to being outside the college, watching it burn down.

Titling a story isn't easy either. The title for this – "Two Villains, a Notebook, and a Lump of Coal" – is part-description of the story, and part-lie. The villains aren't really villains, the notebook is much more than that, and the lump of coal is [SPOILER] something else altogether. Assumptions are dangerous and it can be fun to play with them too.

In the end, I aimed for a story that was part-darkness, part-hopeful future. I want to leave readers with the idea that Leora can go on to live a good life, even if we're not there for it. I think I managed that.

A question for the author

Q: What's easier for you - imagining a happier world, or a darker one?

A: It's easier for me to imagine a darker world - but I'd much rather imagine a happier one. I like my stories, whether I'm writing or reading them, to have at least a glimmer of hope within them, though that can be tough in the very shortest of shorts.

I enjoy all sorts of fiction, and I don't shy away from exploring dark worlds. But I think that even the darkest, grimmest landscape can contain moments of joy or happiness or kindness.

Isn't that what we see all around us? Yes, there are lots of horrible things going on in the world, and it sometimes feels like nothing but doom and gloom, but when it comes both fiction and real life I like to hope there's a chance that tomorrow will be a better day. Or that if it isn't, I will find joy in a small part of it.

Writing a happier world can be tough - is such a world going to be solid and believable? Not everything can be fixed. But writing happy moments is usually achievable, though they may not suit every story.

Writing darkness is usually easier, I just don't want to linger in it for too long.

About the author

Helen French is a writer, book hoarder, TV-soaker-upper, digital project executive and biased parent who grew up in Merseyside and now lives in Hertfordshire, UK. You can find her on Twitter at @helenfrench.

Snapped Dry, Scraped Clean

Setsu Uzumé

Once the corpse is ready to return to the desert, it falls to me to gather her memories. The house where they fester has good bones, but its guts are in turmoil. A stain that looks like bile has seeped through the floor. That means many hours taking up the boards and hauling them to the firehouse. Hours of exposure. Any strong back can haul for the death carts, but carters can't do their work until I finish mine.

Some of the carters still call me Mother Hrisa, though I haven't been a surgeon in twenty years.

Sunlight falls from the window slats onto a clay bowl of chicken stew, alive with maggots. A breath of sadness grazes my cheek and I turn, holding out the vial. The vial shivers, consuming a regret over the uneaten meal. A grunt of discomfort from the other side of the house, and I hold out the collecting vial, moving past the array of octagonal mirrors meant to shine light into the cool, windowless bedroom.

My nose and throat clamp shut against the death smell; a ferment of sweat and bowel. The body must have been left long enough for birds and lizards to puncture the organs. The workers tasked with removing the body for burial were either new, overworked, or both—not bothering to scoop up what leaked out and smeared in their wake. Such smears are breeding pools for infection, even without the danger of the dead's memories to contend with.

It was cleaner when the *ghilan* ranged the sands, loping approximations of humans that ate our dead flesh and dead memories, leaving the living free to move on. The desert made them, and the desert swallowed them forty years ago. Without them on hand to dispose of bodies, we've had to invent new ways to protect the living from the dead. Thats when we started using collecting vials.

There are no candle stands or hand-lamps by the bed. She died alone, encased in darkness.

In ten or fifteen years, this is how I would prefer it, too.

My colleagues were surprised when I announced my resignation from surgery. I had saved many, taught many; but death is like the dust storms. Breezes, siroccos, sandstorms like razors in your eyes, this is the natural flow. Nothing can stop it, or prevent it. It comes. I knew this, I accepted it, and I had no more room in my hands to hold that pain for others. I could not sit in that moment and provide comfort. Forty years of wailing, of births and breaks, fevers, and fears. Thousands of voices begging for aid, for comfort, for release. I was not enough. I couldn't win. I learned to perceive the dead, and turned to this work a decade ago. For solace. For silence.

I see to the dead, because I can no longer bear the living.

I hear wrenched, hacking coughs; but not with my ears. Eyes watering, I reach out with the vial, a thin silver tube just longer than my palm. The name of the deceased, and the family to whom her memories now belong, have been acid-etched into the side. One soul, one vial, one purpose.

My mind is uncluttered, and open. Once I understand the memory, it's a matter of threading sympathy into a lure, and down in to the vial it goes.

...sleep sweet, my little one, see you in the morning sun...

My thumb covers the slender silver container with a *thup* and the memory goes silent. Some families fear secrets more than curses. This takes care of both. The vial gleams, reflecting all that's left of the sun's glory bouncing from mirror to mirror.

I cough, dampening the bandages over my mouth. Ears ringing, I return to the light of the sitting room. I thought the cough caused it, but the ringing grows into pressure. The pressure becomes a sweet scent, slipping in between the filth.

Sweet, but not food. New, but intimately known, an instant rapport like the first smile from someone who truly understands you. The sympathetic resonance of these memories is strange, slightly off; the right tune on the wrong strings. A knowing, rather than perceiving. It snuck in, beneath all the other smells, and sleepless nights, and interminable cries, and nestled among the memories that lingered in the remains.

There are two souls here. This vial can only protect me from one.

Across the room, my supply cart rustles. A bottle of disinfecting tincture falls off and rolls under a chair. Two brushes clatter to the floor.

Where is she? comes a strong little voice.

The vial nearly leaps from my hand. That is not the old woman I was sent here to collect.

Where is my mommy?

I squeeze the collecting vial, now full of the dead woman.

"Shes safe," I call, trying to find the source. "Where are you, little one?"

The floor shudders. Beyond the back doors, the garden is still. The stalks do not waver, the sand doesnt shift. The shaking is only within the house.

Where? demands the little voice. *Im cold, Im scared, Im real!*

One hand firmly clamped over the collecting vial, I dash for the cart, cursing my ancient knees. The shaking becomes more violent, and several more bottles of solvents and disinfectants fall off the cart and shatter, adding the piss-smell of ammonia to the mélange.

Bring her back! Im scared! the sweet voice twists sour, its plump tones stretching and straining, thinning like desiccated flesh left in the open desert, waiting for a *ghilan* to eat and give it rest.

My knees are on fire. I cannot risk injuring myself here, alone, work unfinished; and I have no tools to collect this spirit. I gasp through the pain in my joints, grab the vials amberwood case, abandon my cart, and hobble toward the door. Just as I pull it open, the floorboards buck, ejecting me from the house and throwing me to the ground. The amberwood case skids across the sand. I crawl toward it, then turn over, facing the house. With the vial clutched to my chest, the horrible ringing pulses, slows, and dies.

I tug the wrapping off my face, cough, and spit onto the sand. A spasm shoots painfully through my hip and makes my cheek twitch. My hands shake as I unlock the case and seal the collecting vial inside.

I wonder how the family will lie about this.

The appointment with the family had been set for the following morning on the rooftop portico of my offices. The air scours off the death smell, and sunlight tends to set the mourners at ease. The amberwood case rests on the table, next to a quote detailing a room-by-room cleaning assessment and any relevant amendments requested by the death cart and sanitation workers; a tidy accounting of the spiderweb of reciprocal contracts that characterizes our greatest institutions.

When the family arrives, Deshrin, a gentleman of fifty years and graying temples inclines his head toward me. "I wish to express my gratitude for this meeting, Hrisa."

I nod but do not rise. "I wish to express my great sympathy for the loss of your mother, Deshrin."

His wife, Keprie, and their daughter take their seats next to him. The girl might be fifteen, and the veil she wears across her face is a fashion I thought had died out. The women's hands crossed in their laps, holding their mourning kerchiefs. There is comfort, in grief, to ruin something beautiful, but the kerchiefs' intricate, brightly colored embroidery is completely clean. They were not close.

"Your kind words alleviate the pain in our hearts. Thank you." He pulls his sleeve back with one hand and lifts the teapot, pouring a cup for me. The appropriate deference due to a woman of my eighty-four years, despite the nature of our business. Someone raised him correctly.

"Tell me, when you requested my services, it was solely for your mother, correct? There were no companions, no trusted servants or anyone else to be collected?"

"No, she lived alone." Deshrins eyes narrow.

"Im afraid there has been a complication." I gesture to the quote, and Deshrin takes up the paper. I lift my teacup and sip while he reads.

Deshrin's gaze flicks across the document. His breath catches in his throat when he reaches the middle of the page. "A second? What is—who else is there?" he asks.

"Your sister, perhaps. Once I had collected the last memories, a child made itself known. Perhaps it was shocked to suddenly find itself alone. It is not unprecedented, but it will require extra work; up to and including a second vial. I presume you know the danger if this is not addressed."

Deshrins shoulders slump, and Keprie takes the quote from him to examine it. "This nearly doubles the original price."

"Lower your voice," Deshrin says. "We cannot pay this. Not on record. We cant have any record of a soul left uncollected for so long. What is she, buried in the floorboards? The shame would ruin us and destroy the value of the property."

I hate their voices. I need an apprentice to handle this for me. Even as I look at their faces, all I can see are the shapes of their skulls beneath their skin—the flesh like a mask to be discarded.

"How could this have happened? How could you not know?" Keprie demanded.

After the drought, and the famine, there was a typhoid outbreak. Too many people clustered in the city looking for help. We had to burn bodies en masse. They were dying too quickly for the *ghilan* to eat, and lingering spirits spread everywhere. I lost whole families, entire extended households to disease caused by the uncollected dead infecting their kin. Those that didn't die of illness went insane and took their own lives, spreading to others. We couldnt stop the dead, but we could stop those with infected minds from spreading disease with their corpses. I could tolerate the smell, like cheese left to rot in a pit latrine; but the sound... dry bones snapping like kindling. That, I will never forget.

I gave my life to my work rather than having a family, and that saved me; but not from failure. Healers can only delay death, not stop it; and new parents will say the kin-oath to a newborn, flown spirit or not.

I put my teacup back on the table. "With no more *ghilan* to eat the bodies and souls as one, we are left with the tools at hand."

Keprie pours more tea, speaking softly. "Then your mother was...?"

"Actually insane. Because of the spirit," says Deshrin. "I thought she was just... self-serving."

"Such infections can account for a difficult manner or chronic illness." The next, I say with the detachment appropriate to our profession, but it feels more like bracing for a blow. "Your mother has been collected, and whatever she did to keep her childs spirit contained is no longer in place. Without her, the child's spirit will try to cling to another."

"A sister," Deshrin murmurs. "I never knew."

He could have said anything at that moment and it would have been the same. He reaches for solace and finds none. His wife doesnt move, nor his daughter. No wonder the little spirit didn't infect anyone but its mother. The family are as detached as those in my profession.

"I will do as you ask, and no less," I say. "The rest is up to you."

Deshrin collects himself. "What about the public record? Can we keep a second vial quiet?"

"Thats not exactly legal," I say, stiffly. "The *ghilan* can no longer be relied upon to... return the forgotten to the sand. Your grandchildren would be at risk."

Families can be far-reaching, and so can the impact of an uncollected soul. An inaccurate death record could lead to false evidence or inaccurate court proceedings for generations—on top of any consequences to reputation. Vast amounts of treasure could be wasted trying to correct a mistake that was already accounted for.

"Which means yes, for the right price." Keprie purses her lips.

I incline my head, confirming her assertion. It is an apologetic gesture, as formalized as the bribery itself. "Lineage is both a matter of pride, and of public order."

He assents, but makes a show of blustering anyway. "It never ends. Even in death she subjugates everyone around her. Her secrets become my shame to carry, and Ill be condemned as an inattentive heir."

"So?" says the girl.

Deshrin and Keprie turn to their daughter — whose name escapes me — as though only just remembering she was there. Her voice is strong and clear, despite the modesty of her veil; but the words are garbled, as though they scarcely make it out of her throat. "Eh eer. Ea ah whoo be beh oo-ih." The girl gestures to herself, then Keprie. "I owe. Ma owe." She jabs her pristine handkerchief toward me. "Fee owe."

Keprie offers an embarrassed nod by way of apology, and then translates. "She said, shes here, and she has to be dealt with. She knows, I know, and pardon me, you know, Hrisa." Keprie pats her daughters leg. Then aside, to her daughter, "Dont be rude, Yerdra."

Yerdra. Named for her grandmother. Perhaps a peace-offering between the dead woman and her son.

Deshrin shook his head. "That woman was a tyrant. We owe her nothing."

A futile one.

"The property is a valuable asset," Keprie says. "If we get the house we may recover the losses."

"Of course, with my familys reputation at stake, your only concern is that house."

"Someone has to think of these things," she retorts. "Where do you think the second vial will come from? Those expenses will need to be expunged as well."

I hold a hand up. "I have made my recommendation. You may safely take another day to decide. I can see you have much to discuss."

"Uh och. Gama och," Yerdra says. She makes a gesture of giving, aimed at me.

"What box? Everything in that house is already accounted for in the will," says Keprie.

"She might have one or two small items we could offer in trade for a second vial. She never liked anyone poking about her things," Deshrin mutters.

"I owe weh," Yerdra insists.

Despite her imprecise words, she speaks slowly, filling in the missing consonants with the tone and pitch of her voice.

I know where, she says.

"Youre not going in that house until its been cleansed," Keprie insists. "Leave this for the adults to decide."

Yerdra is a common name, and I've met many Yerdras. I have delivered Yerdras, held Yerdras while their husbands bled, and guided Yerdras into the arms of silence. I wonder about this one.

"Were you close with your grandmother?" I ask.

She rolls her eyes. "Oh," she says. *No.* Children don't typically speak at these meetings, and she has not brought spare paper to write out her thoughts. She speaks again, supplementing her words with gestures. Though Im starting to understand, her mother interprets, speaking over her rather than for her.

"She only visited once, when she was eight. Thats when she found the box she means to offer you, and she didnt go back after that."

Frustration slows Yerdras words even more, but her meaning is clear. *You didnt let me.*

With that, the girl storms out, with Keprie close on her heels.

Now I know this Yerdra. And her parents surprise when they saw her cleft lip and palate. I wonder who decided on the veil.

Deshrin presses his hands together. "I would like meet her, just for a moment, when shes collected."

"Uncollected dead cause disease." I drop my finger onto the relevant line item of the invoice. "As part of your services, there will be a sitting to review your mothers collected memories before the last mourning day."

"But we wont get that with my sister if shes off the record," he counters. "Youll be there. If she will not speak, you can collect her before she harms us."

He wants to reopen the wound so it might heal cleaner. To feel like hed done something, even if it was too little, too late. I dont want to feel his pain. My skin crawls. I want to leap out of my chair and run, but I sip my tea and compose myself.

"The invoice will need to be adjusted, to make sure youre fitted with safe clothes."

He grimaces, but nods. We set a time to meet at the house, and he departs.

Im going soft. I sip my tea.

Perhaps, to the deceased Yerdra, chaining her baby's soul to her and accepting the risk of dementia felt less insane than putting that empty husk on a bonfire. Clinging to the loss, being hollowed out by it for that long, any person would crack and shatter.

Human beings are not collecting vials.

Keprie, Deshrin, and Yerdra arrive carefully wrapped in surren silk, a pale-yellow fabric that protects the skin from exposure to unclean material. They assure me they received my message and have worn clothes that they are prepared to throw away in the event they accidentally touch conventional filth. I wouldn't have them risking consumption or cholera through negligence. I show them how to wrap the surren to prevent gaps as an extra measure against infection. With the house still befouled, I carefully inspect their shoulders, elbows and fingers to make sure they can still move without putting themselves at risk.

Once inside, I sprinkle the floor with disinfecting powders and give the maggoty pot to the drowned garden, breaking off the few tall stalks left standing. Today there are two cases on my cart. A second vial has been acquired and brought to the house, a lower-grade silver, and lacking the family crest. It is a courtesy, to keep their secret and privacy.

Inside, Deshrin wrings his hands, looking up at the domed ceiling. "Hrisa, when will—how will she—do we call to her?"

"Memories are difficult to catch in company," I reply. "Try to make yourself quiet. Hold your feelings at a distance."

"A distraction, then," said Keprie. "You said there was a box, darling. Something valuable. Where did she keep it?"

In there, Yerdra says, pointing at the bedroom.

"That area is not safe to enter," I remind them. "The remains have not been properly disposed of."

"Youve been in there," Keprie says. "Are we not wrapped the same way?"

"Such sights are disturbing. If you vomit in your wrappings you would need to go outside to dispose of them, and I will not permit you back in," I say.

Yerdra puffs air dismissively and pushes past me.

Deshrin and Keprie start moving choice pieces of furniture to the back garden to sun-bake, and I follow Yerdra into the dark.

She moves lightly through the cluttered space, long and deft as a needle, avoiding contact with the foulness in the room. She is almost blue here, less solid than the outside world of brown stalks and orange sand.

Yerdra stumbles, and glass shatters. A dozen glass bottles had fallen to the floor —nestled into the folds of a table linen that slipped from its place. By the smell, medicine for pain.

"Are you cut? Your shoe?" I ask.

"Uh-uh." She bends over a writing desk, peering at a half-written letter.

"Can you breathe? The smell—"

She tugs her mask down for a moment —a foolish thing to do, in this filthy room —but the moment is enough. Her mouth looks as though it has been slashed upward into each nostril. "I kah fme." *I cant smell.*

She watches me, challenging me to wince or look away.

The sick, the elderly, the damaged—they terrify the living. Yerdras face must be no different. Maybe her parents veiled her to hide from their own mortality.

The dying do the same, curling up in darkness and denial, not wanting to trouble anyone, including themselves.

Yerdra tugs her mask back up. The watering in her eyes is the same as mine; the body cleansing itself of death, whether it can smell or not.

She points to the desk. "Afe?"

"Yes. Only ink," I reply.

She swallows, then traces one finger along the underside of the desk. She fumbles with a mechanism, and then *click, slide,* a secret drawer. She pulls out a box made of small, faded green stone. Octagonal. Something rattles inside it.

It is very difficult to understand her, but I listen. I find myself using the same tendrils of sympathy I use in my work to peel back the layers of meaning within the sounds she makes. She is frustrated at her parents. She disagrees with their approach; but it's more than the chafing and flippancy of one her age. There are pinpricks of regret in what she's conveying, new understanding, and wrongdoing.

We should have been here, she seemed to say. This Yerdra turns, moving the box out from under her shadow and into the scant light. *We should have asked.*

A subject that must have been dear to her, having to measure the worth of her words against the value of paper.

"Whats done is done," I say. I have no wish to use the sympathetic technique with a living person. It is too painful. The effort of listening to her speak, and the care with which she tries to be understood — it feels the way healing felt. The same intimacy dregs up my time in surgery. I don't want it. Her words burrow into buried places like worms.

It is not my concern. It is my job to cleanse, not to comfort. Not anymore.

"Cleaners are in the business of preserving dignity. Distance is kindness." I shift away from her and my boot rasps against a sheaf of discarded parchment on the floor. "Death's shadow is long, yet new babies arrive nearly every day."

I recall the many that didn't. When the mothers wailed, rather than the children.

"Kin dont abandon kin." She squeezes the box for a moment, like she might throw it. Then she presses the box into my hand. "Here. For the vial."

She returns to the hosting room, and I fiddle with the lid in the dim light, feeling for the catch. It twists, and then opens.

Inside is a small, grey-green stone, thick at one end, tapering at the other. I squint at it.

Its a *ghilan* tooth.

A big molar. I thought they were all gone. Ground up and carefully processed, this could make thousands of collecting vials — or, in the right hands, perhaps we could find out why they disappeared.

"Where did she get this?" I ask, but Yerdra has gone toward the back gate already.

"Yerdra?" I call.

A breeze slips through the window slats and rustles a bit of paper to the floor. The air takes on weight; it hurts my back. I dart into the light of the main room to check on the family. Keprie touches her temple.

Mommy? asks the little voice.

The realization hits me like the death-smell. Yerdra. The spirit heard her mother's name.

That pressure again, like last time. It moves from my ears to my chest.

I curse myself for my sloppiness. The little spirit was waiting for us, and I woke her up too soon.

Deshrin darts inside from the garden, calling to me for help. "Hrisa!"

I rush toward the cart, the vial, but pain shoots through my knee and I stumble. The house trembles, the chipped red cup smashes on the ground. Across the room from me, Yerdra drops to the floor, choking.

"Stop!" I cry, but I feel as though my lungs are being squeezed.

Yerdra convulses, beyond my reach.

Its so warm, a heartbeat again! Dont take her away, the little voice says, to me. *Im real, Help me!*

"You cant have her, she isnt your mother!" I sputter.

Mommy dont leave me, dont lock me away, Im real! The pressure in the air becomes heavier. My back and shoulders ache, and my knees burn as I try to stand. Yerdra rolls to one side, hunching, yellow ichor leaking into the wrappings over her mouth, nose, and ears. She was the only one not protected by detachment. Yerdra was the only one who cared enough about the dead woman for the little spirit to see her. The child's spirit recognized only her as family, and it is killing her. I had heard of this happening, but misjudged the strength of its hunger. I cannot lose against death again.

I am already old.

I have been hollowed out by the lives I could not save. I had room within my mind to trap her. All I needed was the right lure.

"You are not real!" I cry. "You have never had, or lost. You do not know what it is to be alone!"

I scrape out the last of my humanity and offer it in trade. I could not stop death, and she had never lived. Each of us has only the memory of closeness, the longing for it. We are at two ends of the same rope, fraying and rotten. If I can convince her to see me as family—as the mother she lost—I can use that rope to pull her into my mind.

Or, the rope could snap. But I am out of options. If my life ends today, let me delay anothers death one last time.

I become a vial, and call the little spirit into me. She answers.

Show me.

My lungs and throat burn. My eyes swim and my stomach turns. The last thing I see is Yerdra roll onto her stomach.

All at once, the little one is here. She is a weight and a lightness in my mind. Every whisper that I thought long buried rushes up to meet her. Every dancing laugh and crash of sorrow tangles her consciousness with mine. She rakes and sifts through my memories, tasting and pawing, recoiling and savoring them. Time bends and stretches, and I see her as my child might have been. I watch her grow into a young healer, always at my side. Then shes grown, no longer my shadow but my equal when I quit the hospital. They call her mother, as I was called mother. Through me—with me—she bears witness to a thousand births, and a thousand deaths. She stands sentinel over the ill and the injured, and holds space for the sad and afraid. The little spirits voice—not mine—whispers somewhere between my ears and my memory:

I swear to protect you and care for you, I swear to nurture and bestow my strength unto you, I swear to let no one bring you harm who does not first bring harm to me. From my first breath to your last, I swear that you are my kin.

The kin oath, what parents say to their children before their naming, ripples through my mind. The little spirit shows me what roused her. Deshrin and Keprie teasing each other while sandscrubbing dishes. Yerdras surprise when I dont flinch at her face. Then, my office a few weeks ago, giving instructions to my staff and the way they trust me. The sun's rays gleaming from mirror to mirror, lighting up the bedroom at just the right time. With each scrape, the boundaries between the little spirit and me snap apart. With each snap, I feel something crack and shatter. She is within me, the little spirit; holding my hand. The gnarled roots of my failings seem to loosen and recede, scouring the doubt and regret that had calcified around them. My lifetime becomes hers. She becomes part of me— and I am enough.

The cascade of memory eases and drops me back into the now. The house, the family, my aching knees. I push myself up to a sitting position on sand, not floorboards. They have pulled me outside.

I cough and spit.

"Hrisa?" says Keprie. "I did not see you close her in a vial. Is it done?"

Our wrappings have been stripped off, and the antiseptic smell of the surren silk lingers on my hands. Yerdra holds the octagonal box with the tooth. I must have dropped it.

Deshrin helps me to my feet. My hands tremble.

"Are we safe?" Deshrin asks.

The little spirit should have killed me. I do not know why she didnt.

"Yes." I put my hand over my heart, and feel something nestle in, like a child curling against me to sleep. "The child has been collected."

"The rock?" Yerdra asks, her voice a little thick from her ordeal.

Keprie wrinkles her nose, "what rock?"

"A curio from a darker time," I say, taking the box from Yerdra. "If youll allow me to have it, the bill and public record will remain unaltered."

"Yes, agreed," said Deshrin.

"I will stay." Yerdra spits into the sand. "I will help."

"The carters will return tomorrow just after dawn to finish the cleaning. I hope youre prepared to pull up floorboards," I say.

She smiles, eyes flinty. Her teeth glint through the crests of her upper lip.

Perhaps she could be taught to handle invoices.

The family prepares to depart, changing out of their protective wrapping and into clean clothes. I lean on the outer wall of the house, and the breeze kicks dust over the dunes. I feel lighter, and heavier, the ragged edges of my failures relived, and then relieved. I open the box again and consider the *ghilan* tooth, heavy with possibility. I wonder if the little spirits presence within me will shorten or extend my life, and if theres time to make more vials, or train others to hear and collect spirits. Or perhaps, to find the *ghilan* and return them to their lands, freeing human hands from this burden. I consider the weight of them both: the tooth and the little spirit, and whether collecting the secrets and memories of the dead prepared me to survive this ordeal.

I wonder how many vials my death will require.

But for now, my heart is fuller, and my failures quieter. That quiet changes how I hear the family taking their leave. Their chatter is the clatter of a busy kitchen, the creak of doors after a long day, and the murmuring of sorrows shared and laid to rest. It whispers across the sand, glimmers in the sun, and then finally, blows away.

See Setsu Uzumé's story "Snapped Dry, Scraped Clean" online at Metaphorosis. If you liked it, leave a comment. Authors love that! Remember to subscribe to our e-mail updates so you'll know when new stories are posted.

About the story

This story came out of two news articles I read in 2014. The first was about the biohazard techs who clean up crime scenes in New York, and the second was about a woman whose body was discovered in the stairwell of a San Francisco hospital. Providing care is hard, but sometimes receiving care is harder.

A question for the author

Q: What do you think makes for a good story?

A: Voice. Voice is like the truth, but its flavored by awkward, embarrassing, and messy realities — not what you think the audience wants to hear. It gives insight and context that shapes everything else. Voice is the thing that makes a story different and interesting, the same way a person stands out when they represent themselves authentically. It isnt always easy. Part of voice is exposing our hopes and fears to the scrutiny of strangers; but to me thats what makes a story come alive.

About the author

Setsu Uzume is the host and assistant editor at *PodCastle*. Setsu writes and occasionally narrates dark fantasy. They are taking a break from sword work to study horseback archery. While they have dabbled in many arts, only writing and martial arts seem to have stuck.

katanapen.wordpress.com, @KatanaPen

Copyright

Metaphorosis Publishing

Metaphorosis offers beautifully written science fiction and fantasy. Our projects include:

Metaphorosis Magazine

Metaphorosis, a weekly magazine of SFF short stories, including stories from all the authors in this anthology. Find out more at magazine.metaphorosis.com, and sign up to be notified of new stories.

Metaphorosis Books

Recent books from Metaphorosis can be found at <u>books.metaphorosis.com</u>, and include:

Metaphorosis 2017

Metaphorosis 2016

All the stories from *Metaphorosis* magazine's second year.

Almost all the stories from *Metaphorosis* magazine's first year.

Metaphorosis:
Best of 2017

The best science
fiction and fantasy
stories from
Metaphorosis' 2nd
year.

Metaphorosis:
Best of 2016

The best science
fiction and fantasy
stories from
Metaphorosis' 1st
year.

Reading 5X5

Reading 5X5

Five stories, five times

Twenty-five SFF authors, five base stories, five versions of each – see how different writers take on the same material.

Writers' Edition

All the stories from the regular, readers' edition, plus two extra stories, the story seed, and authors' notes.

Best Vegan SFF of 2017

The best vegan science fiction and fantasy stories of 2017!

Best Vegan SFF of 2016

The best vegan science fiction and fantasy stories of 2016!

Susurrus

A darkly romantic story of magic, love, and suffering.

www.ingramcontent.com/pod-product-compliance
Lightning Source LLC
Chambersburg PA
CBHW020529120726
47904CB00003B/1008